MW00947647

THIS BOOK BELONGS TO

INDEX

TEST COLOR PAGE

WRITE DOWN YOUR FAVORITE ASPECTS OF THIS BOOK

Thank you very much

for trusting and choosing our product

Wish you all the best in your future

Hope you will put your trust in our next product.

Made in the USA
Columbia, SC
04 September 2024

41608296R00059